Karen Lee Baker

SENECA

Greenwillow Books, New York

For Paul

*Special thanks to Robin Roy
and Barbara Russell*

Watercolor paints were used to create the full-color artwork. The text type is Veljovic.

Copyright © 1997 by Karen Lee Baker. All rights reserved. No part of this book may be reproduced or utilized in any form or by any means, electronic or mechanical, including photocopying, recording, or by any information storage and retrieval system, without permission in writing from the Publisher, Greenwillow Books, a division of William Morrow & Company, Inc., 1350 Avenue of the Americas, New York, NY 10019.

Printed in Hong Kong by South China Printing Company (1988) Ltd. First Edition 10 9 8 7 6 5 4 3 2 1

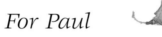

LIBRARY OF CONGRESS CATALOGING-IN-PUBLICATION DATA

Baker, Karen, (date)
Seneca / by Karen Lee Baker.
   p.   cm.
Summary: After choosing a horse for her own, a young girl takes care of it, goes for rides, and visits it each day.
ISBN 0-688-14030-0   [1. Horses—Fiction.]   I. Title.
PZ7.B17426Se   1997   [E]—dc20   95-35846   CIP   AC

When I met Seneca, I was looking for a horse of my own.
He had a friendly face and soft brown eyes. He seemed
happy to see me.
I held out my hand, then gave him a pat on the neck.

I put Seneca's halter on him and led him into the center aisle.
He followed quietly.
The owner placed a saddle on Seneca's back.
She let me put his bridle on him.
Seneca was not a young horse, but
when I rode him, he was full of
spirit and power. He moved
eagerly from a walk to a trot
to a canter.
I knew at once he was the
horse for me.

His new home is a small barn at the top of a hill.
After school I race on my bike to see him.
"*Neighhhh!*" Seneca usually meets me by the gate.

I give him corn husks, his favorite snack.

There are chores to be done. I clean his stall every day . . .

and fill his bucket with fresh water.

At grooming time I find Seneca dozing in the sun.
He's usually dusty from rolling in the dirt to scratch
that itch on his back.

I loosen the dirt with a curry comb, then hard-brush him all over. When I use a softer brush on his face, he almost falls asleep. Then I use a metal pick to remove the stones and dirt packed in his hooves.

Our fall trail rides in the woods are the ones we like best.
There are no bugs to bother us.

Seneca is very good at dodging trees.

If there is a log in our path, Seneca jumps it eagerly.
Once in a while I'm not ready for the jump . . .

and I lose my balance and fall off.
He always waits nearby.

Often on our rides we pass a cow pasture.
All the cows stop grazing and stare at us.

But Seneca is brave and walks on
with his head held high.

When we come to an open field, he gets excited and so do I.

We gallop away.

Seneca needs some coaxing to walk into the creek.
He hesitates and his ears flicker back and forth.

Once in the water, though, he wants to stay
and splash about.

At sunset our fun is over.
I let the reins hang loose, and Seneca takes me home.

He always knows the way back to his barn.

I remove his saddle and bridle and put him in the paddock.
While he is cooling off, I scoop out his grain.
Seneca whinnies. He knows it is dinnertime.
I throw hay down from the loft for his second course.

Before the day is over, I must rake the aisle.
Then I rest and listen to Seneca munch his hay.

I wish I could stay longer. I give him a hug.
"Good night, Sen. I'll see you tomorrow."

Sometimes he glances over at me while he
eats his hay, as if to tell me the same.

I turn off the lights and close the barn door behind me.
I'll be back in the morning.